Sea of Shadows

Kenneth Haines
Sea of Shadows

—

Published by - Spines
ISBN: 979-8-89569-784-9

Sea of Shadows

A Tale of Love, Loss, and Survival

Kenneth Haines

Contents

The Storm Approaches

A Family Adventure

In the wake of a furious storm that had tossed their boat like a toy in a bathtub, Helene found herself on the shores of a deserted island, the salty air mingling with the scent of damp earth and decaying leaves. As she sat beside her Papa's body, covered in beach sand, grief washed over her like the waves lapping at the shore. Yet, amid the heartache, an indomitable spirit flickered within her. This island, with its wild beauty and harsh realities, was now their world, and Helene felt an innate call to honor her father's memory by embracing the challenge ahead. This was not just a tale of loss, but also one of resilience and the unbreakable bond of family.

As the days turned into weeks, Helene discovered that survival was not merely about finding food and shelter; it was about coming together as a family in the face of adversity. The skills her Papa had taught her in happier times now transformed into lessons of survival. She learned to fish with makeshift nets, forage for edible plants, and build a shelter from palm fronds and driftwood. Each small victory ignited a sense of purpose within her, reminding her that her Papa's teachings would guide her through this storm of life. The island, once a backdrop of despair, became a canvas for her determination and love.

The dynamics of their family began to evolve in surprising ways. Helene's memories of her Papa became a source of strength rather than just sorrow. She often spoke to him as she worked, sharing her thoughts and dreams, feeling his presence in the rustling leaves and the whispering winds. Each evening, she would sit on the beach, looking out at the horizon, where the sky kissed the sea, and she would imagine her Papa's laughter echoing through the waves. This connection bridged the gap between loss and healing, allowing her to navigate the complexities of grief while still feeling anchored to her past.

Nature, too, played a pivotal role in her healing process. The island was a paradox of beauty and brutality, a reminder of life's fragility. Sunrises painted the sky with hues of orange and pink, casting a warm glow that wrapped around Helene like a gentle embrace. The vibrant life surrounding her—colorful birds, lush greenery, and the rhythmic sound of the ocean—reminded her of the resilience of nature itself. She learned to find solace in the simple moments: the feel of sand beneath her feet, the taste of fresh coconuts, and the symphony of the sea. Each day brought new challenges, but it also offered a fresh perspective on life and death, teaching her that healing could coexist with the echoes of loss.

As Helene forged her path through this overwhelming journey of survival, she began to understand that family bonds could transcend even the most profound grief. The island became a testament to her Papa's legacy—a place where love endured, where memories intertwined with the very fabric of the earth. With every step she took, she carried him with her, a constant reminder that they were forever connected. This family adventure on a deserted island was not just about survival; it was about learning to thrive amidst loss, embracing the beauty of life, and finding hope in the depths of despair. In the heart of the Sea of Shadows, Helene discovered her strength and the transformative power of love, forever etching her family's story into the sands of time.

THE UNEXPECTED TEMPEST

The wind howled like a wild beast, its fury echoing through the desolate landscape as Helene sat beside her father's lifeless form. The storm that had torn through their lives had arrived without warning, a tempest that transformed a serene day at sea into a harrowing struggle for survival. As she looked at the sand that covered him, a mixture of grief and determination surged within her. She knew she had to honor his memory by finding the strength to endure, even in the face of overwhelming despair. The island, though unforgiving, became both a sanctuary and a battleground, forcing Helene to confront the raw elements of nature and her own heart.

The chaos of the storm had stripped away the layers of comfort that once surrounded their family. It was just Helene now, a young girl grappling with the loss of her father and the reality of being stranded. Yet, in this stark isolation, she discovered that survival was not merely about physical endurance; it was also about emotional resilience. The lessons her father had imparted on fishing, foraging, and navigating the seas echoed in her mind, guiding her as she sought to transform her grief into a will to live. Each day became a testament to their bond, a silent promise to carry his spirit with her as she learned to navigate the challenges of the unforgiving island.

Nature, with all its chaotic beauty, became a profound teacher. Helene found solace in the rhythmic crash of the waves and the rustle of palm leaves swaying in the breeze. The island, once a place of fear, began to reveal its secrets. She learned to identify edible fruits, to catch fish in the shallows, and to build shelter from the elements. In her solitary moments, the vibrant colors of the sunset painted across the sky reminded her that even in loss, there was beauty to be found. Each sunrise offered a new chance to honor her father's legacy, to embody the adventurous spirit he had instilled in her. The very nature that had once threatened them now became a source of healing and strength.

As days turned into weeks, Helene's understanding of family dynamics evolved. The loss of her father shifted her perspective, making her reflect on the bonds that tied them together. Memories of laughter, lessons learned, and moments of tenderness floated to the surface, reminding her that love transcends even the most profound loss. She began to visualize her family as a guiding force, their voices echoing in her mind, urging her to keep moving forward. In this journey of survival, she learned that the essence of family could never be lost; it transformed, adapted, and continued to nurture her spirit in ways she had yet to fully comprehend.

The unexpected tempest had not only claimed her father but had also ignited a fierce determination within her. As she stood on the shore, the ocean stretching endlessly before her, Helene realized that she was part of something much larger than herself. The island, with its wild beauty and harsh realities, had forged her into a survivor. In every challenge she faced, she felt her father's presence, guiding her through the shadows of despair towards the light of hope. With each passing day, she embraced the duality of grief and healing, understanding that it was in the depths of loss that she could truly learn to live.

The Struggle for Survival

The relentless crashing of waves against the shore echoed the chaos that swirled within Helene's heart as she sat beside her Papa's lifeless body, now a part of the very sand that had once cradled their laughter. The storm had stolen everything—her family, their boat, and the very essence of safety that had wrapped around them like a warm blanket. Yet, even in the clutches of despair, there remained a flicker of hope, an ember that refused to be extinguished. Nature, in its raw beauty and unforgiving cruelty, offered both a grave reminder of loss and a powerful impetus for survival.

As the sun dipped below the horizon, painting the sky in hues of orange and purple, Helene felt the weight of solitude pressing down on her. She knew that survival was not just a physical battle against the elements but an emotional struggle that required resilience and tenacity. In her heart, she vowed to honor her Papa's memory by embodying the strength he had always believed she possessed. With every breath, she began to forge a plan, drawing on the survival strategies she had learned from countless family camping trips. She recalled the lessons of building shelter, finding fresh water, and foraging for food, each a thread woven into the fabric of her upbringing.

The island, with its jagged cliffs and dense foliage, was a living entity, sometimes hostile, often indifferent, yet it pulsed with life. Helene understood that she needed to engage with this environment, to listen to its whispers, and to find ways to coexist amidst the pain. Each day became a journey of exploration, where the ocean provided fish and the trees offered fruits. In her quest for sustenance, she discovered not only the physical resources necessary for survival but also the healing balm of nature that began to mend the fractures within her heart.

As days turned into weeks, Helene found herself reflecting on her family dynamics, recalling the warmth of shared meals and the comfort of whispered secrets. The memory of laughter echoed in her mind, reminding her that survival was not merely about enduring alone but about connection, even in the absence of those she loved. She began to create rituals that honored her family—gathering shells to represent each member, lighting a small fire as a beacon of hope. In doing so, she transformed her grief into a source of strength, forging an unbreakable bond with the memories that would forever guide her.

In the end, Helene's struggle for survival became a testament to the resilience of the human spirit. The island had become both her sanctuary and her adversary, a place where she learned to navigate her sorrow and embrace the possibility of new beginnings. Through the lens of loss, she discovered the profound truth that healing often comes not from forgetting, but from remembering, cherishing, and ultimately, transforming that loss into a foundation for a future filled with hope. Each sunrise became a reminder that even in the darkest moments, life could emerge anew, vibrant and unyielding, and that the love she carried would forever guide her through the shadows.

The Aftermath

Awakening Alone

As the first rays of sunlight broke through the dense canopy of palm trees, Helene stirred from her slumber, the gentle rustle of the waves lapping at the shore stirring her from a dreamless sleep. The world around her was a tapestry of blues and greens, yet it felt surreal and detached. She blinked, her mind clouded with confusion, and then the memories crashed down like a wave—a storm, the frantic cries of her family, and the unmistakable weight of loss. As she sat up, her heart ached with the reality that she was alone, perched beside her Papa's body, now covered with beach sand. It was a moment suspended in time, where grief and survival intertwined, forcing her to confront the rawness of her existence.

In that moment of profound loneliness, Helene felt the island breathe around her. The chirping of birds, the whispering wind, and the distant crash of waves were a chorus of life that surrounded her in stark contrast to her inner turmoil. Nature, in its indifferent beauty, became both a balm and a challenge. She understood that to survive, she had to immerse herself in this world, to learn its rhythms and heed its lessons. The island was not just a backdrop; it was a teacher. As she gathered the courage to rise, Selene felt the weight of her Papa's teachings echoing in her heart—resilience, resourcefulness, and the unyielding bond of family, even in death.

Survival strategies began to take form in her mind as she surveyed her surroundings. Food and fresh water were her immediate concerns, but beyond that, she knew she needed a plan to honor her Papa's memory while ensuring her own survival. She remembered the stories he used to tell about foraging and fishing, about the importance of shelter from the elements. With each small task—collecting coconuts for hydration, fashioning a makeshift fishing line from twine—Selene began to reclaim her agency. She was not merely a victim of circumstance; she was a survivor, and the island became her crucible, shaping her into someone stronger than she had ever imagined.

In this solitary struggle, Selene also began to explore the depths of family dynamics through the lens of loss. The echoes of laughter shared with her Papa now merged with the stark silence of the island, creating a poignant contrast that drove her forward. Each step she took, each decision she made, was influenced by the love and lessons he had imparted. She learned to carry him with her, weaving his spirit into the fabric of her survival. The connection to her family transcended the physical realm; it became a guiding light, illuminating the path ahead even when darkness threatened to engulf her.

Nature, in its vastness and unpredictability, played a crucial role in healing Selene's heart. The crashing waves that once symbolized turmoil now offered a soothing rhythm, a reminder of the cycle of life and death. Each sunrise brought with it a new chance to embrace her grief while pushing forward. The island wasn't just a place of despair; it was a sanctuary for renewal and growth. As she forged through the wilderness—gaining strength and wisdom—Selene discovered that love, though often tied to loss, could also be a powerful motivator for survival. It was in embracing both her sorrow and her resilience that she found her true self, standing unwavering against the backdrop of the Sea of Shadows.

Grief and Despair

Grief is an uninvited companion that often accompanies loss, wrapping around the heart like a heavy shroud. In the aftermath of the storm that claimed Selene's family boat, she finds herself stranded on a deserted island, a place that is both hauntingly beautiful and mercilessly isolating. Perched beside her Papa's lifeless body, covered with the coarse, unforgiving beach sand, Selene is consumed by a profound despair. Yet, even in this darkest moment, there is a flicker of resilience that begins to emerge. It is in the depths of her sorrow that she discovers an innate strength, a survivor's instinct that urges her to honor her father's memory by forging ahead.

Nature, with its raw beauty and unyielding force, becomes both a backdrop and a catalyst for healing in Selene's journey. The rhythmic sound of the waves crashing against the shore serves as a haunting lullaby, reminding her of the life that once thrived within her family. As she navigates this desolate landscape, Selene learns to find solace in the very elements that once threatened her existence. The gentle rustle of palm fronds, the vibrant colors of the sunset, and the starlit sky above her become her companions, whispering promises of hope amid the shadows of grief. In her exploration of this untouched paradise, she begins to understand that even in loss, nature holds the power to mend the broken pieces of the heart.

Survival strategies emerge not only from physical needs but also from the emotional landscapes that families traverse in the wake of tragedy. Selene, though alone, draws upon the lessons her father imparted during their time together – the importance of resourcefulness, gratitude, and the strength of familial bonds. Each day becomes a testament to her determination to survive, as she forages for food, collects rainwater, and builds a shelter. Yet, it is the memories of laughter and shared stories that fuel her spirit, reminding her that family is not merely defined by presence but by the indelible marks they leave on our souls.

The dynamics of family in survival narratives reveal profound truths about love, loss, and resilience. Selene's connection to her Papa transcends the physical realm; it is woven into the very fabric of her being. As she faces the challenges of island life, she recalls the moments of tenderness shared between them, the lessons learned around the campfire, and the stories that brought them closer. Each memory acts as a lifeline, keeping her anchored amid the turbulent seas of despair. In recognizing the strength derived from these familial ties, Selene learns to navigate her grief, transforming it into a source of power that fuels her will to survive.

Ultimately, Selene's journey through grief and despair becomes a testament to the healing journey that follows loss. Embracing her sorrow allows her to honor her father's legacy while also forging a new path forward. As she learns to coexist with her grief, she uncovers the beauty of resilience and the transformative power of love. Nature, a constant presence, becomes a nurturing force in this process, reflecting the cycles of life and renewal. In the depths of despair, Selene discovers that even amid the shadows, there is light to be found, guiding her toward a future where hope and healing can coexist with the memories of the past.

A New Reality

In the heart of an unrelenting storm, the world as Selene knew it had crumbled. Stranded on a deserted island, the roaring waves that had once seemed like a playful lullaby now echoed as a haunting reminder of the tempest that had claimed her family boat. The soft grains of sand, now a blanket over her father's still form, felt both comforting and cruel, a stark juxtaposition of life and death. As the sun broke through the parting clouds, casting golden rays upon the desolate shore, Selene found herself at the crossroads of grief and survival. This new reality, harsh and unforgiving, demanded strength she never knew she possessed.

In the silence that enveloped her, Selene reflected on the life lessons her father had imparted during their countless adventures on the open sea. He had taught her to navigate not only the waters but also the storms of life. Each wave crashing against the shore was a reminder that nature's fury could be both destructive and transformative. With every breath of salty air, she felt the weight of responsibility settle on her shoulders. Survival was no longer just about enduring the elements; it was about honoring the legacy of love and resilience her father had instilled in her. It was time to rise, not just for herself, but for the memory of the family they had been.

As days passed, Selene began to forge a new path amidst the desolation. With each sunrise, she ventured into the lush greenery that surrounded her, learning to read the language of the island. The rustling leaves whispered secrets of edible fruits, while the distant call of birds guided her to fresh water. She became a student of survival, transforming her grief into determination. Each small victory—finding sustenance, creating shelter, and mastering the art of fishing—reinforced her belief that even in the depths of despair, hope could sprout like wildflowers through cracks in the earth.

The solitude of the island presented Selene with an unexpected gift: the opportunity to explore the dynamics of family and loss. Memories of laughter echoed in her mind as she recalled the stories shared under starlit skies. In those moments of reflection, she understood that her family's love would always be a part of her, a guiding light in her darkest hours. The island, once a symbol of isolation, transformed into a canvas where she could paint her grief into something beautiful. She began to see the natural world as a healing force—a sanctuary where she could confront her pain, allowing the gentle rhythm of the waves to soothe her troubled heart.

With each passing day, Selene embraced her new reality, recognizing that survival was not merely a physical challenge but an emotional journey. The island became her teacher, imparting wisdom about resilience, the power of nature, and the enduring nature of love. As she continued to navigate the complexities of her loss, Selene emerged not just as a survivor, but as a beacon of hope for others who might one day find themselves in similar circumstances. In the depths of her sorrow, she discovered the strength to honor her father's memory, forging a new identity rooted in courage and the unwavering belief that love could transcend even the most devastating of storms.

Selene's Resolve

Embracing the Challenge

In the heart of despair, where the horizon met the endless sea, Selene found herself in a place that tested the very fibers of her being. The storm had come like a thief in the night, robbing her of safety, comfort, and the laughter of her family. Now, as she sat beside her Papa, his body gently cradled by the soft sand, she felt the weight of grief pressing down on her. But among the shadows that enveloped her, a flicker of strength began to ignite. It was in this moment of profound loss that Selene realized embracing the challenge of survival was not merely about enduring; it was about honoring the love that had shaped her life.

Survival strategies emerged not only from instinct but also from the lessons her Papa had imparted throughout their lives together. As the sun dipped below the horizon, casting long shadows across the beach, Selene recalled their family outings, where her father taught her to read the tides and understand the language of the waves. With his memory as her guide, she began to assess her surroundings, gathering resources from the island. Every coconut cracked open, every fish caught, was not just an act of survival but a tribute to the bond they shared. In each challenge she embraced, she felt his spirit urging her onward, reminding her of the resilience that lived within them both.

The dynamics of family, especially in extreme situations, reveal the depth of love and connection that often goes unspoken. As Selene navigated the difficulties of her new reality, she found herself reflecting on the moments that had defined her family. The laughter during shared meals, the stories exchanged under starlit skies, and the lessons learned through trials were woven into the fabric of her existence. Each memory became a source of strength, a reminder that even in loss, the essence of those we love remains alive within us. As she engaged with the challenges of survival, Selene understood that she was not alone; her Papa's love was her compass, guiding her through the darkest days.

Nature, in its raw beauty and unforgiving power, played a pivotal role in Selene's journey of healing. The island was both a sanctuary and a crucible, offering solace amid the storms of grief. The sounds of the waves crashing against the shore became a soothing melody, washing over her, reminding her of the cycle of life and death. Each sunrise brought new colors to the sky, a promise of hope and renewal. As she learned to coexist with the land and sea, Selene discovered that nature was a reflection of her own resilience. The very elements that had once brought destruction also offered the gift of rebirth, teaching her that healing often comes from embracing the challenges that life presents.

Embracing the challenge of survival transformed Selene from a girl lost in sorrow into a beacon of hope and strength. As she lit her first fire, its flames flickering against the encroaching darkness, she felt a profound connection to her Papa, to the love that would never fade. Each day became an opportunity to honor his memory through her actions, to carve a new path forged by determination and the unbreakable bond of family. In the face of overwhelming odds, Selene discovered that within the depths of her sorrow, there was also the potential for growth, healing, and a renewed appreciation for the beauty of life. Through embracing the challenge, she became not just a survivor, but a testament to the enduring power of love amidst the shadows.

MEMORIES OF PAPA

Memories of Papa enveloped Selene like the warm rays of the sun breaking through the clouds after a storm. As she sat beside his body, covered in the soft, golden grains of beach sand, she could almost hear his laughter mingling with the rustling leaves and the gentle lapping of the waves. Her mind drifted back to the days before the storm, when their family boat sailed smoothly across the shimmering sea, and Papa's steady hand guided them through both calm waters and turbulent tides. He had always been the anchor of their family, a source of strength and wisdom, teaching her not just to navigate the ocean but to navigate life's unpredictable currents.

In those fleeting moments, Selene remembered the countless survival strategies he had imparted to her—how to read the stars, how to find fresh water, and how to build a shelter from the elements. Each lesson was imbued with his love, a testament to the bond they shared. Now, stranded on this deserted island, those teachings echoed in her mind, urging her to summon the resilience that Papa had always believed she possessed. With every wave that crashed onto the shore, she felt his spirit urging her to survive, to thrive even in the face of overwhelming loss.

The island, a stark contrast to the vibrant world she once knew, offered her both solace and challenge. Nature's beauty was a balm for her grief, reminding her of the lessons her father had imparted about finding hope in the midst of despair. The rustling palm fronds whispered secrets of survival, and the salty breeze carried with it the essence of life. In this harsh yet beautiful environment, Selene learned to forage for food and purify water, skills she never thought she would need. Each small victory felt like a tribute to Papa, a way to honor his memory while forging her own path.

Family dynamics took on a new meaning as her thoughts turned to her mother and brother, lost in the chaos of the storm. The bond they shared was tested, yet Selene felt a calling to keep their memory alive, to embody the love and strength Papa had instilled in them. In the quiet moments, she envisioned them together, laughing and telling stories around a fire, which fueled her determination to survive not just for herself, but for the family they had been. She realized that survival was not merely about enduring; it was about nurturing those connections that defined who they were.

As the sun dipped below the horizon, painting the sky in hues of orange and purple, Selene closed her eyes and inhaled deeply, allowing the scent of the ocean to wash over her. She felt Papa's presence with her, guiding her through the darkness of grief towards the light of hope. In every wave that crashed and every star that twinkled above, she found comfort and inspiration, knowing that his love would forever be her compass. The memories of Papa, woven into the fabric of her being, became the foundation upon which she would build her new life, embracing the journey of healing and survival with a heart full of love.

Finding Strength in Vulnerability

In the stillness of the deserted island, surrounded by the relentless sound of waves crashing against the shore, Selene discovered a profound truth: vulnerability can be an unexpected source of strength. As she sat beside her Papa's body, covered in the gentle embrace of beach sand, she felt a wave of sorrow wash over her. Yet, within that grief lay the seeds of resilience. The rawness of her emotions connected her deeply to the land, reminding her that even in the face of overwhelming loss, there is space for healing and growth. It was in her moments of despair that she began to understand the power of embracing one's vulnerability, a lesson that would guide her through the trials of survival.

As she navigated the challenges of isolation, Selene recognized that vulnerability is not a sign of weakness but a bridge to authenticity. Stranded on an island, far from the comforts of home, she confronted her fears and doubts head-on. Each day presented new obstacles, from finding food to constructing shelter, but with each hurdle, she learned to lean into her feelings rather than suppress them. Acknowledging her pain allowed her to tap into an inner well of courage that she never knew existed. This journey through her emotions became a survival strategy, equipping her with the clarity to make decisions that would ensure her survival while honoring her Papa's memory.

In the heart of nature, Selene found solace and strength. The island, with its untamed beauty, mirrored her own tumultuous journey. The roar of the ocean became a soothing lullaby, and the rustling leaves whispered tales of endurance. Nature, in its raw form, offered her not only comfort but also inspiration. As she observed the resilience of the flora and fauna around her, struggling yet thriving in the harsh environment, she began to see her vulnerability as a form of strength. The island taught her that survival isn't just about physical endurance; it is also about emotional resilience, about allowing oneself to feel deeply and to rise despite the odds.

Family dynamics often shift dramatically in times of crisis, and Selene felt the weight of this truth as she grappled with her loss. Her relationship with her Papa had been one of mutual respect and love; now, it was a memory that defined her reality. The bond they shared became the foundation upon which she built her strength. As she recalled their conversations, the lessons he imparted, and the love they shared, she realized that vulnerability could forge deeper connections even in absence. It was through her grief that she felt his presence most keenly, guiding her as she navigated the treacherous waters of survival.

In embracing her vulnerability, Selene emerged transformed. The experience taught her that acknowledging pain can pave the way for healing and personal growth. As she continued to confront the challenges her new life presented, she found strength not just in her solitude but in the memories of her family. The island, once a place of despair, became a sanctuary where she learned to integrate her loss into her survival narrative. In this sea of shadows, she illuminated a path toward resilience, honoring her past while forging ahead with newfound courage and hope.

Survival Strategies

Foraging for Food

Foraging for food in the wild can be a daunting task, especially when one is faced with the reality of survival on a deserted island. For Selene, perched beside her Papa's body, the world had transformed into a blend of grief and necessity. As the waves lapped at the shore, she realized that her connection to the land would serve as both a lifeline and a bridge to healing. In this fragile moment, the island revealed its bounty, offering her the chance to honor her father's memory by embracing the very instincts he had nurtured in her throughout their adventures together.

The first step in foraging is to observe the environment. Selene's keen eyes scanned the sandy stretches and rocky outcrops, searching for signs of life. She remembered her Papa's lessons about the importance of patience and awareness in nature. With each small discovery—a cluster of wild berries here, a patch of edible seaweed there—she felt a flicker of hope. These small victories became her source of strength, reminding her that even in the depths of despair, the earth could provide sustenance and comfort.

As she ventured further along the shoreline, Selene discovered the art of gathering from the sea. Shellfish nestled in tide pools and crabs scuttling across the rocks became part of her new reality. The rhythm of the waves was a soothing backdrop to her efforts, allowing her to momentarily escape the weight of her sorrow. In this way, the act of foraging evolved into a ritual, a means of connecting with her father's spirit while also nurturing her own resilience. Each morsel she collected was infused with love and remembrance, transforming her grief into a celebration of life.

The process of foraging also deepened Selene's understanding of family dynamics in the face of adversity. She imagined her Papa beside her, guiding her hands as they explored together. Their shared experiences of fishing, gathering, and cooking had forged an unbreakable bond. Now, as she foraged alone, Selene realized that she was not just surviving for herself but also for him. Her determination to thrive became a tribute to their connection, weaving the lessons of their past into the fabric of her present.

Ultimately, foraging became a path toward healing for Selene. Each discovery allowed her to channel her grief into something tangible, transforming loss into a newfound appreciation for life. As she prepared her meals with the fruits of her labor, she felt a sense of empowerment wash over her. In the embrace of nature, surrounded by the elements that had once brought her joy alongside her father, Selene found a way to navigate her sorrow. The island, in its raw beauty, became a sanctuary—a place where love and loss intertwined, offering her the strength to move forward, one step at a time.

CREATING SHELTER

Creating shelter is not just a matter of survival; it's an act of hope and resilience, a tangible expression of love for those we hold dear. In the wake of a storm that has ravaged the familiar and left only the unknown, Selene finds herself on the edge of a deserted island. Beside her, her Papa lies covered in beach sand, a stark reminder of the fragility of life. Yet, in this moment of despair, the instinct to create a safe haven emerges as a powerful testament to human tenacity. Building shelter becomes a way for Selene to honor her father's memory and shield her heart from the relentless waves of grief and uncertainty.

As Selene surveys the island, she observes the resources around her. The fallen palm fronds, sturdy driftwood, and abundant foliage whisper the promise of safety and warmth. Each piece of material holds a story, a potential for something greater. With every branch she gathers and every palm frond she weaves, Selene channels her energy into a craft that transcends mere survival. She is not just creating a physical barrier against the elements; she is constructing a cocoon of comfort that reminds her of home, of laughter shared, and of the love that still lingers in her heart.

In the solitude of the island, Selene discovers that shelter building is as much a physical endeavor as it is an emotional journey. Each knot tied and every layer stacked symbolizes her determination to endure. The act of creating a space where she can mourn and remember becomes a ritual of healing. As she works, the rhythmic sound of the waves offers a soothing backdrop, a reminder that nature, while fierce, can also be a source of solace. The shelter begins to take shape, a reflection of her inner strength and a sanctuary where she can process her loss amidst the beauty of her surroundings.

Family dynamics shift dramatically in extreme situations, and Selene's relationship with her Papa becomes a guiding force. Memories of their adventures together fuel her resolve to build a shelter that embodies their shared spirit of exploration. She recalls the stories he would tell, the lessons he imparted about resilience and adaptability. With every decision she makes—what to use, how to position the shelter—Selene feels his presence guiding her hand. This connection transforms her grief into a powerful motivation, reminding her that love can transcend even the most harrowing of circumstances.

As the sun sets over the horizon, casting a golden hue over her makeshift shelter, Selene takes a moment to reflect. The structure stands not only as a physical barrier against the elements but as a symbol of survival and healing. It is a place where she can honor her Papa's legacy, a sanctuary where she will gather her strength to face the challenges ahead. In this quiet space, surrounded by the whispers of nature and the memories of love, Selene understands that even in the depths of loss, there is room for hope, and from the shadows of despair, she can emerge into the light of a new beginning.

NAVIGATING THE UNKNOWN

In the heart of adversity, where the horizon meets the relentless waves, Selene finds herself enveloped in a profound silence, the kind that follows great loss. Her father, once a pillar of strength and guidance, now rests beneath a fragile mound of sand, the world around him a stark contrast to the chaos that had just unfolded. Stranded on a deserted island, she feels the weight of survival pressing down on her, yet within that weight lies an unexpected opportunity for resilience. As she gazes at the ocean's vastness, Selene realizes that navigating the unknown is not merely about physical survival; it is also about embracing the emotional journey that accompanies such profound loss.

In the days that follow, every sunrise becomes both a reminder of her father's absence and a symbol of hope. Each wave that laps at the shore whispers stories of survival, urging her to find strength in vulnerability. Selene begins to understand that survival strategies extend beyond the practicalities of shelter and food. They delve deep into the psyche, exploring the family dynamics that shape how individuals cope with loss. She recalls the stories her father shared of their ancestors, resilient families who faced storms of nature and life, drawing strength from one another. In her solitude, those tales transform into guiding stars, illuminating a path through despair.

Selene learns to navigate this new world with the instincts her father had instilled in her. She scavenges for coconuts and edible plants, each bite a small victory against the gnawing hunger that threatens to overwhelm her. Yet, as she gathers resources, she also cultivates memories, letting the laughter of shared meals and the warmth of family moments guide her hands. The island becomes her classroom, teaching her not just how to survive, but how to thrive amidst the memories that envelop her. With each day, she begins to see that even in the darkest moments, hope can take root, nourished by the love that remains.

Nature, in all its beauty and brutality, emerges as a powerful force in Selene's healing process. The rustling leaves and the calls of distant birds become a soundtrack to her grief, reminding her that life continues unabated. Each storm that rolls in brings with it a fierce reminder of her father's teachings about respect for the sea and its power. As she stands against the wind, she feels a connection to him, as if he is guiding her through the tempest of emotions. The island, with its lush landscapes and hidden dangers, becomes a living testament to her journey—an embodiment of loss, yet also a cradle for her spirit to mend.

In the end, navigating the unknown transforms from a daunting challenge into a profound journey of self-discovery. Selene learns that survival is not just about enduring the physical challenges of a deserted island; it is about embracing the emotional currents that flow through her. The love for her father becomes a beacon, illuminating her path forward, while the lessons learned amidst the shadows of loss empower her to face each new day with courage. In the depths of her heart, she understands that while the island may have claimed her father, it has also become a sacred space for her to honor his memory and forge a new life, reminding her that even in the face of overwhelming darkness, the light of love endures.

The Healing Power of Nature

Connecting with the Ocean

In the quiet aftermath of the storm, as the sun began its ascent over the horizon, Selene found herself perched beside her Papa's body, the grains of beach sand gently cascading over him like a soft, protective shroud. The rhythmic sound of the waves lapping against the shore offered a sense of comfort amidst the overwhelming grief. In that moment, the ocean transformed from a fearsome adversary to a nurturing presence, reminding Selene of the deep connections that bind us to nature and to those we love. It was as if the sea was beckoning her to remember the laughter they shared, the lessons learned, and the resilience forged in the face of adversity.

The ocean, with its vastness and unpredictability, serves as a powerful metaphor for life's challenges. For families stranded in extreme situations, the water can be both a source of sustenance and a reminder of survival's fragility. As Selene navigated the shores of her grief, she began to see the ocean not just as a barrier, but as a vital resource. Gathering driftwood for shelter and collecting rainwater, she learned to adapt to the rhythms of her surroundings. Each small victory in her quest for survival became a connection to her Papa's teachings, reinforcing the wisdom he imparted about respecting nature and harnessing its gifts.

In the face of loss, Selene's journey also illuminated the intricate dynamics of family bonds. The ocean, with its ebb and flow, mirrored the complex emotions swirling within her. She recalled her Papa's stories of survival, shared around campfires under starlit skies, where the sea was both a background and a character in their family narrative. These memories became a lifeline, reminding Selene of her Papa's strength, resilience, and unwavering love. As she embraced the elements, she discovered that the spirit of her family lived on in the very air she breathed and the waves that danced along the shore.

Nature, in its raw beauty, plays a crucial role in the healing process. For Selene, each encounter with the ocean was a step toward reconciliation with her grief. The salty breeze brushed against her skin, whispering secrets of resilience, while the tide washed away her tears, leaving behind a sense of renewal. The ocean taught her that loss is not an end but a transformation, a passage that could lead to deeper connections with both the past and the present. In observing the way the sea nurtured life, she began to see her own potential for growth amidst the shadows of her sorrow.

Ultimately, connecting with the ocean became a profound journey of self-discovery for Selene. It was a reminder that even in the most challenging circumstances, there exists an opportunity for healing and hope. The ocean's vastness reflected her own capacity to endure, to learn, and to love despite the pain of loss. As she embraced the beauty and challenges of her surroundings, Selene understood that the spirit of her Papa would forever accompany her, guiding her through the tides of life. In the embrace of the ocean, she found not only solace but also a renewed sense of purpose, ready to honor her family's legacy and navigate the uncharted waters ahead.

THE COMFORT OF THE WILD

The island enveloped Selene in a cocoon of tranquility, a sharp contrast to the chaos that had consumed her life only days before. As she sat beside her Papa's body, covered gently with beach sand, she felt the pulse of the wild around her. The rhythmic crashing of waves created a haunting melody that resonated within her, a reminder of the life that once thrived alongside her beloved father. In this serene yet stark setting, Selene began to understand that the wild could offer more than just survival; it could provide comfort in her grief and a path toward healing.

Nature has an incredible ability to cradle the broken-hearted. The vibrant hues of the sun setting on the horizon filled Selene's heart with a bittersweet beauty. Each color painted across the sky was a reflection of the love she held for her family, a love that would never fade despite the void left by loss. The rustling leaves and whispering winds seemed to echo her tears, telling her that she was not alone. The wild embraced her sorrow and transformed it into a shared experience with the world around her, reminding her that life goes on even in the face of devastating loss.

In such an extreme situation, survival strategies extended beyond the physical aspects of finding food and shelter. Selene learned to navigate her grief through the very elements that surrounded her. Fishing became a ritual, a way to honor her Papa's teachings, while gathering fruits from the island's trees reminded her of family gatherings where laughter filled the air. Each task was infused with memory, transforming survival into a sacred act of remembrance. The island, though a place of solitude, became a canvas where she painted her survival story with strokes of resilience and love.

Family dynamics often shift dramatically in times of crisis, revealing the strength of bonds that can be both fragile and unbreakable. As Selene faced the harsh realities of her new existence, she found herself reflecting on the lessons her Papa had instilled in her. The love between them served as a guiding light, illuminating her path as she learned to adapt to her surroundings. In conversations with the waves and the trees, she discovered that her family was not merely a memory but an enduring presence that continued to guide her instincts and decisions.

Ultimately, the wild became a sanctuary for Selene, a place where she could confront her grief while embracing the beauty of each new day. It taught her that loss is an integral part of love, shaping her into someone who could withstand the storms of life. In the heart of the wilderness, she found the courage to carry her Papa's spirit forward, forging a new identity grounded in both loss and survival. The comfort of the wild was not just in its natural beauty, but in its ability to nurture the human spirit, allowing her to heal and grow amidst the shadows of her past.

Nature as a Teacher

In the wake of grief, nature stands as a silent yet powerful teacher, guiding those who are lost through the labyrinth of their emotions. As Selene sat beside her Papa's body, the rhythmic sound of waves crashing against the shore became a haunting lullaby that echoed the love they shared. The gentle breeze caressed her face, whispering tales of resilience and hope. In that desolate moment, surrounded by the vast expanse of the ocean, she felt an undeniable connection to the world around her—a world that mirrored her own turmoil yet offered the promise of healing. Nature had a way of showing that even in the depths of despair, life continues to pulse and thrive.

Survival on a deserted island requires more than just physical endurance; it demands an understanding of the natural world that surrounds us. As Selene navigated her new reality, she learned to observe the rhythms of nature, recognizing the patterns of tides and the behavior of animals. Each day was a lesson, teaching her how to forage for food, find fresh water, and build shelter, all while honoring the memory of her father. The island became an unintentional mentor, revealing secrets that would help her survive and thrive. In every challenge, the landscape offered solutions, turning her grief into a source of strength as she embraced the raw beauty of her surroundings.

Family dynamics shift dramatically in the face of survival. For Selene, the loss of her Papa created an emotional chasm that seemed insurmountable. Yet, nature provided her with a unique perspective on their bond. Each sunrise painted the sky with colors that reminded her of the stories he used to tell, instilling a sense of continuity in her life. The lessons of love and sacrifice he imparted were etched in her heart, guiding her through the loneliness of loss. As she learned to fend for herself, she realized that the essence of her family was not lost; it transformed, becoming a part of the very air she breathed and the earth beneath her feet.

In the struggle for survival, Selene discovered the healing power of nature. The island was not merely a backdrop to her grief; it became a sanctuary where she could confront her emotions in their rawest form. The gentle rustle of leaves and the distant calls of seabirds provided solace in her solitude. Each day, she would sit by the shore, allowing the ocean's rhythm to wash over her, granting her the space to grieve and heal. Nature, in its unyielding beauty, taught her that loss is a part of life and that every ending paves the way for new beginnings. As she embraced this truth, she found herself slowly mending, learning to carry her father's spirit within her as she forged ahead.

Ultimately, Selene's journey on the deserted island became a testament to the profound relationship between nature and the human spirit. She emerged from the shadows of her loss, equipped with survival skills that transcended mere physicality. The island taught her not just how to survive but how to thrive in the face of adversity. In every challenge she overcame, she found a piece of her father, a reminder that love endures even in the most desolate of places. Through the wisdom of nature, Selene transformed her grief into a source of strength, embodying the enduring lesson that in the heart of darkness, the light of hope can still shine brightly.

Family Dynamics in Crisis

Roles and Responsibilities

In the heart of despair, where the horizon meets the endless expanse of the ocean, the roles and responsibilities that emerge in times of crisis can redefine the very essence of family. As Selene sat beside her Papa's body, covered with the soft embrace of beach sand, she felt an overwhelming weight of responsibility settle upon her young shoulders. In that moment, she transformed from a girl into a protector, understanding that her role extended far beyond mere survival. It was about honoring her father's legacy while navigating the treacherous waters of loss and uncertainty. Each decision she made carried the weight of love and remembrance, illustrating how the bonds of family strengthen in the face of adversity.

In the struggle for survival on a deserted island, every family member must embrace their unique role to contribute to the collective effort. For Selene, this meant becoming a resourceful problem solver, using her creativity to devise strategies for finding food and shelter. Her Papa had always taught her the importance of ingenuity, and now, she applied those lessons with a fierce determination. The island, with its lush greenery and hidden dangers, transformed into a classroom where she learned to adapt and thrive. This shared responsibility not only fostered resilience but also deepened the connection between her and her Papa, even in his absence.

As the days turned into weeks, the dynamics of family life shifted dramatically. Selene found herself not only mourning the loss of her father but also stepping into a nurturing role for her younger siblings. The act of caring for them became both a burden and a balm, as it allowed her to channel her grief into something meaningful. The responsibilities of leadership and protection became intertwined with moments of joy and laughter, reminding them all of the love that still lingered in the air. Through this process, they discovered that their roles were fluid, each sibling rising to meet the challenges and support one another in their darkest hours.

Nature, too, played a pivotal role in their journey of healing and survival. The island, once a source of fear and isolation, gradually became a sanctuary of solace and strength. Selene learned to listen to the whispers of the wind and the rhythm of the waves, finding comfort in the natural world around her. The responsibilities of survival were balanced by the healing powers of nature, which offered both sustenance and serenity. Each sunrise brought new opportunities for growth, while the stars at night reminded them of their Papa's enduring spirit, illuminating their path even in the depths of sorrow.

Ultimately, the tales of love, loss, and survival woven into their experience illustrated the profound impact of roles and responsibilities within a family. In the face of overwhelming challenges, Selene and her siblings discovered the strength that lay within their connections to one another and to the world around them. As they navigated the complexities of grief and survival, they realized that their responsibilities were not merely tasks to be completed, but threads that bound them together in an unbreakable tapestry of resilience. Through love, they forged a path toward healing, proving that even in the darkest of times, the human spirit can endure and flourish.

The Bond of Shared Struggles

In the quiet aftermath of the storm, as the sun began its slow descent into the horizon, Selene found herself in a moment suspended in time. The island, with its rugged cliffs and whispering winds, stood as a stark contrast to the turmoil within her heart. Beside her lay her father, a figure once so vibrant and full of life, now transformed into a memory draped in beach sand. The weight of loss was heavy, yet amidst the sorrow, Selene felt an undeniable bond forming, not just with her father through shared memories but also with the very nature surrounding her. It was in this desolation that she discovered the resilience of the human spirit and the profound connections that emerge against the backdrop of shared struggles.

Survival on this deserted island demanded more than just physical endurance; it required a deep emotional strength. Selene recalled the countless times she and her father had navigated challenges together, their laughter echoing in the face of adversity. Those moments of shared struggle had forged an unbreakable bond, a tapestry woven from love, patience, and understanding. As she faced the daunting task of surviving alone, she realized that the lessons learned during those times would guide her. Each wave that crashed against the shore reminded her of her father's teachings, urging her to adapt, to be resourceful, and to find hope amidst the chaos.

In the hours that followed, Selene began to explore the island, searching for food and shelter. The tasks were physically demanding, but they offered her an opportunity to channel her grief into action. Nature became both her companion and her teacher, revealing the bounties of the land and the rhythm of survival. With every fruit she found and every shelter she built, she felt her father's presence, encouraging her to embrace the challenges ahead. The bond they had formed through their shared struggles was now a guiding light, illuminating her path forward, reminding her that love transcends even the boundaries of life and death.

As days turned into weeks, Selene learned that healing from loss is not a linear journey but a winding path marked by moments of reflection and renewal. Each sunrise brought a new chance to honor her father's memory, and each sunset allowed her to release her grief into the gentle embrace of the ocean. The island, once a symbol of her despair, transformed into a sanctuary of healing. In the stillness of the night, as the stars twinkled like distant memories, Selene felt a sense of connection not only to her father but to the very essence of life itself. The struggles she faced were now a testament to resilience, binding her to the earth and the spirit of her family.

Ultimately, Selene's journey on the deserted island became a profound exploration of family dynamics in the face of adversity. The bond forged through shared struggles became a source of strength, reminding her that even in loss, love is a powerful force that endures. Nature played its role in her healing, providing solace and strength, teaching her that every challenge can be met with courage and grace. As she stood on the shores, gazing out at the endless sea, Selene understood that the journey of survival was not just about overcoming hardship; it was about embracing the legacy of love, honoring the memories that shaped her, and finding hope in the shadows of despair.

COMMUNICATING THROUGH GRIEF

In the heart of the storm, when the world outside rages and nature's fury swells, there exists a profound silence within the soul. Selene, perched beside her Papa's body, feels the weight of loss heavy in the air, yet there is a gentle whisper that reminds her of the love they shared. Grief is a powerful force, one that can either engulf us or lead us to deeper understanding. In the midst of despair, communication becomes a lifeline, not just with the memories of those we have lost but also with ourselves, the very essence of who we are in the face of adversity.

On a deserted island, surrounded by the vastness of the sea, the struggle for survival takes on a new dimension. For Selene and her family, every moment spent in the fight for life is intertwined with the threads of their collective grief. As they navigate the challenges of finding food and shelter, they also confront the emotional turmoil that comes with loss. Open conversations about their feelings bring them closer together, allowing them to share stories, laugh through tears, and honor the memory of the one they lost. This form of communication not only bridges the gap between sorrow and healing but also fortifies their bond, turning their grief into a source of strength.

Nature, with its wild beauty and unforgiving realities, plays a crucial role in this journey of healing. The rhythmic sound of waves crashing against the shore becomes a backdrop to Selene's reflections, a reminder that life and death are intertwined like the tides. Each sunrise offers a new beginning, a chance to embrace the fleeting moments and to cherish the connection they shared with her Papa. As she learns to fish and forage, Selene finds solace in the natural world; it becomes a nurturing space where her grief can coexist with the joy of survival. The island, once a setting of despair, transforms into a sanctuary where she can communicate her feelings not only to her family but also to the universe around her.

Through storytelling, families can transform their grief into something tangible. Selene's tales of her Papa's courage and kindness serve as a beacon of hope for her family. In sharing these stories, they create a legacy that outlasts the physical loss. Each narrative woven through their days on the island becomes a thread that binds them, allowing the family to process their emotions collectively. The act of remembering becomes an essential survival strategy, reinforcing their love and commitment to one another as they navigate the uncharted waters of grief together.

Ultimately, communicating through grief is not merely about expressing sorrow; it is about embracing the complexities of love and loss. As Selene gazes across the horizon, she understands that her journey is one of resilience, where nature, family, and memory intertwine. In this sea of shadows, she learns that while the pain of loss may never fully dissipate, the love shared can illuminate the path forward. Together, they will forge a new existence, where grief is honored, stories are shared, and survival is enriched by the bonds of family and the healing embrace of the natural world.

Moments of Hope

Finding Joy in the Little Things

In the midst of despair, when the world feels like it has crumbled into an endless sea of shadows, finding joy in the little things can become a lifeline. Selene, perched beside her Papa's body covered with beach sand, had to confront the harsh reality of loss while navigating the desolate island. Yet, amidst the sorrow, she discovered glimmers of beauty that punctuated her grief. Each wave that kissed the shore became a reminder of the life that once pulsed through her family, and each grain of sand that slipped through her fingers whispered stories of resilience. In these moments, joy wasn't about grand gestures, but rather the subtle reminders that life, even in its fragility, continued to offer small gifts.

As Selene explored the island, she found that the vibrant colors of the sunset painted the horizon with hues of hope. The laughter of a distant bird or the gentle rustle of palm fronds in the breeze became a melody that lifted her spirit. These elements of nature, often overlooked in the chaos of everyday life, transformed into symbols of survival, teaching her that joy could coexist with sorrow. Each discovery—a unique shell, a hidden cove, or the intricate patterns of leaves—served as a testament to her ability to adapt. This newfound appreciation for the little things became a source of strength, propelling her forward in her journey of healing.

In the years to come, Selene would reflect on how these moments of joy helped her navigate the complex emotions that accompanied her loss. Families stranded in extreme situations often face the challenge of maintaining their bonds as they confront adversity, and Selene's experience was no different. The shared laughter that erupted over a small catch of fish or the warmth of a shared blanket under the starry sky reinforced the connection between her and her Papa. These instances of joy, however fleeting, served as a reminder that love could still thrive amidst grief, creating a foundation for resilience in the face of overwhelming challenges.

The role of nature in healing from loss cannot be understated. As Selene walked along the shoreline, the rhythmic sound of the waves became a balm for her aching heart. Nature, with its cycles of birth, death, and rebirth, mirrored her own journey through grief. Observing the resilience of the island's flora and fauna, she learned to find strength in vulnerability. Each blossom that unfurled in the sun brought a flicker of hope, teaching her that joy could emerge from the ashes of sorrow. This connection to the natural world not only anchored her in the present but also paved the way for future growth and healing.

Ultimately, finding joy in the little things became Selene's guiding principle, a beacon of light in her darkest moments. As she learned to appreciate the simplicity of life on the island, she recognized that these small joys were not just distractions but vital components of her survival. They nurtured her spirit and reminded her of the beauty that remained in the world, even after profound loss. In the end, Selene's journey was not just about survival; it was about embracing life with all its complexities, treasuring the fleeting moments that brought joy, and understanding that even in the depths of sorrow, the heart has the capacity to heal and find light once more.

Signs of Resilience

In the heart of despair, amidst the vast emptiness of a deserted island, signs of resilience emerge like fragile blooms against the harshest of landscapes. Selene, a young girl perched beside her Papa's body, covered in beach sand, embodies the raw strength that life demands in the face of tragedy. As she gazes at the horizon, the relentless waves whisper tales of survival, urging her to find solace in the world around her. Each breath of salty air is a reminder of the bond they shared and the lessons her father imparted, igniting a flicker of hope that life, however altered, must continue.

Resilience often reveals itself in the small, everyday acts of survival. For Selene, each day becomes a testament to her resolve as she navigates the challenges of the island alone. She learns to forage for food, discovering edible plants and fishing in the glistening tide pools. With each successful catch, she not only nourishes her body but also her spirit, transforming grief into determination. The island, once an ominous prison, slowly morphs into a classroom where she learns the art of survival, drawing strength from her environment and the memories of her father's teachings.

Family dynamics shift dramatically in the face of adversity, often unveiling hidden depths of character and connection. As Selene grapples with the loss of her father, she recalls the stories they shared, the laughter that echoed through their boat during calm seas, and the lessons of courage he instilled in her. These memories become her guiding stars, illuminating the path forward. In her solitude, she discovers that resilience is not solely about enduring hardship but also about cherishing the love that survives beyond loss. The island, with its quiet beauty, becomes a canvas for her healing, allowing her to reflect on the love that will forever anchor her heart.

Nature plays a pivotal role in this journey of healing, serving as both a challenge and a comfort. The sun rises and sets, marking the passage of time, while the gentle rustle of palm leaves offers a lullaby to soothe her restless thoughts. Each encounter with the vibrant ecosystem around her—from the vibrant colors of the fish to the soothing sounds of the ocean—reminds Selene that life persists despite the sorrow she bears. The island's beauty acts as a balm, enabling her to remember her father not just in grief, but also in gratitude for the life lessons he imparted.

Ultimately, the signs of resilience are woven into the fabric of Selene's existence as she learns to navigate the complexities of loss and survival. She transforms her pain into purpose, crafting a narrative of strength that honors her father's legacy. As she embraces the rhythm of the island, Selene discovers that within the depths of sorrow lies an unyielding spirit, one that not only survives but thrives. With each passing day, she becomes a testament to the enduring power of love and resilience, forging a new path illuminated by the light of hope that remains ever bright, even in the darkest of times.

BUILDING A FUTURE

In the depths of despair, when the waves of grief crash relentlessly against the shore of Selene's heart, a flicker of hope emerges. The sun, though hidden behind clouds of sorrow, begins to shine through, igniting a determination within her. Stranded on this deserted island, she realizes that survival is not solely about physical endurance; it is about the enduring spirit of family and the connections that bind them. As she sits beside her Papa's body, enveloped in a blanket of sand, she understands that building a future begins with honoring the past. In the face of loss, Selene's journey transforms from mere survival to a quest for meaning, resilience, and love.

Selene reflects on the lessons taught by her Papa, lessons that resonate deeply as she navigates this new reality. Each breath she takes becomes a tribute to his wisdom, a reminder of the strategies they once discussed for overcoming obstacles. She recalls the importance of resourcefulness: gathering food from the land and sea, finding fresh water, and creating shelter from the elements. These survival strategies, once abstract concepts, now manifest as vital tools in her hands. With each task completed, she builds not just a physical existence but also a legacy of hope and strength that honors her family.

The dynamics of family, even in their absence, play a crucial role in shaping Selene's approach to survival. She remembers the laughter they shared, the stories told around the fire, and the unwavering support they provided each other in times of crisis. This bond, though tested by tragedy, fuels her resolve to persevere. Selene realizes that she is not alone in her struggle; the love she feels for her family transcends the physical realm. It is this love that compels her to push forward, to create a future where their memory lives on. In the isolation of the island, she learns that family does not solely consist of those present; it is a tapestry woven from shared experiences and enduring connections.

As Selene forges ahead, she begins to recognize the healing power of nature surrounding her. The rhythm of the tides, the rustle of the leaves, and the songs of distant birds become her companions in grief. Each element of the natural world serves as a reminder of life's continuity, its ability to thrive even amidst chaos. In the gentle embrace of the island, Selene discovers moments of tranquility that allow her to process her loss. Nature, with its inherent cycles of death and rebirth, teaches her that healing is not linear but rather a journey filled with ebbs and flows, much like the ocean waves that cradle the shores of her new home.

With time, Selene begins to envision a future built not on the ashes of her past but on the foundation of resilience and hope. She plants seeds in the fertile soil, both literally and metaphorically, nurturing them with love and intention. The island becomes not just a place of survival but a canvas for her dreams, a testament to her determination to thrive. As she embraces the lessons of loss and the strength of family, Selene understands that building a future is an act of love—a love that endures, evolves, and ultimately transforms the shadows of grief into a brighter horizon.

The Journey Home

A New Understanding of Family

Amidst the relentless waves crashing against the shore, Selene found herself in a world stripped of its familiar comforts, where the very essence of family took on a profound new meaning. As she sat beside her Papa's body, lovingly covered with beach sand, she realized that family is not solely defined by blood or the presence of loved ones but rather by the bonds forged through shared experiences and collective resilience. In that moment of profound loss, surrounded by the unfathomable beauty of nature, Selene began to understand that the essence of family transcends the physical realm; it resides in the memories created and the love that lingers in the heart.

In the face of adversity, families often discover untapped reservoirs of strength and unity. Stranded on a deserted island, Selene learned that survival extends beyond the struggle for food and shelter; it encompasses the emotional ties that bind individuals together. The lessons imparted by her Papa, whether in the form of survival strategies or gentle wisdom, became a guiding light in her darkest hours. As she navigated the challenges of their new reality, Selene recognized that family is a tapestry woven from shared hopes, dreams, and even heartaches. It is in the act of coming together to face the unknown that the true spirit of family reveals itself.

The dynamics of family evolve in extreme situations, forcing individuals to confront their vulnerabilities and strengths. Selene's experience on the island highlighted the importance of communication and collaboration in fostering unity. Without her Papa, she leaned on her instincts and the memories of their time together to guide her actions. In the solitude of the island, she discovered that family can also be found in the connections formed with the environment, as nature became both a companion and a teacher. The rustling leaves, the calls of distant birds, and the rhythm of the tides served as reminders of the life that continues, encouraging her to embrace her role as a survivor.

Nature, in all its splendor and brutality, played a crucial role in Selene's healing journey. The island, though a place of loss, gradually transformed into a sanctuary where she could process her grief and find solace. The vibrant sunsets and the soothing sound of waves became a backdrop for reflection and renewal. In her solitude, she learned to honor her Papa's memory by embracing the beauty surrounding her, symbolizing the cycle of life and death. Each day became an opportunity to connect with nature and herself, allowing her to rebuild her sense of identity and purpose.

Ultimately, Selene's experience on the island redefined her understanding of family as a fluid concept, rooted in love, resilience, and the capacity to heal. It taught her that the bonds of family extend beyond the physical presence of loved ones; they live on through the lessons learned, the memories cherished, and the strength to carry on. Surrounded by the vastness of the ocean and the whispers of the wind, she discovered that even in the depths of sorrow, the spirit of family continues to thrive, guiding the way toward hope and survival.

The Return to Civilization

As the sun dipped below the horizon, painting the sky in hues of orange and violet, Selene sat beside her Papa's body, the gentle waves lapping at the shore. The island, once a place of isolation and despair, transformed into a sanctuary that cradled both her grief and her memories. In those quiet moments, she began to understand the depth of her loss, but also the resilience that lay within her. Nature, with its vibrant colors and soothing sounds, offered a healing balm, reminding her that even in sorrow, there exists the potential for renewal.

Survival on the deserted island was a test of both physical endurance and emotional strength. Selene recalled the lessons her Papa had imparted during their family outings, teaching her the importance of resourcefulness and adaptability. Each day brought new challenges—a hunt for food, the construction of a shelter, and the ever-present threat of the elements. She learned to forage for edible plants and catch fish, skills that would not only sustain her but also honor her Papa's legacy. In those moments of struggle, she discovered an inner fortitude, a sense of purpose that pushed her forward, even when despair threatened to engulf her.

The bond between Selene and her Papa had always been a cornerstone of her life. Now, in the face of unimaginable loss, that bond became a guiding light. Each memory of laughter shared, lessons learned, and stories told became a source of strength. She often found herself speaking to him as if he were still there, seeking guidance from the whispers of the wind and the rustle of the leaves. This connection allowed her to navigate her grief, transforming it into a powerful driving force that propelled her towards survival and, eventually, the hope of returning to civilization.

As days turned into weeks, Selene began to envision a future beyond the island. The thought of reconnecting with the world filled her with both excitement and trepidation. She contemplated the life she had left behind, the family who had been searching for her, and the stories she would share upon her return. In those reflections, she realized that every experience, every moment of hardship, had prepared her for this very journey. The island may have been a place of loss, but it had also given her the tools to thrive, to navigate the intricate dynamics of family resilience in the face of adversity.

Finally, the day came when a ship appeared on the horizon, a beacon of hope cutting through the vast expanse of ocean. Selene's heart raced as she waved her arms, tears streaming down her face. She felt a profound sense of gratitude for the lessons learned and the strength discovered during her time on the island. The return to civilization was not just a physical journey; it was a transformation of spirit. With the memories of her Papa guiding her, Selene stepped forward, ready to embrace the world anew, carrying the echoes of love and loss within her, forever intertwined with the healing power of nature.

Carrying Lessons Forward

In the wake of unimaginable loss, Selene sat beside her Papa, the weight of grief pressing heavy upon her heart. The beach, sun-drenched yet desolate, offered little comfort as the waves lapped rhythmically against the shore. This island, once a mere backdrop for adventure, had transformed into a sacred space, a canvas painted with memories of laughter and love. In that moment, Selene understood that while she had lost her guiding star, the lessons imparted by her father would forever illuminate her path forward.

Survival on the deserted island demanded more than physical endurance; it required emotional resilience and a profound understanding of family dynamics. Selene recalled her father's teachings—how they had worked together to navigate storms, both literal and metaphorical. The bond forged through shared struggles became a lifeline, reminding her that while loss is a solitary journey, the lessons of love and unity can unite even the most fragmented spirits. She resolved to carry those lessons forward, not only for herself but as a tribute to her father, ensuring that his legacy would endure in every decision she made.

Nature, with its raw beauty and unyielding power, became both a teacher and a healer for Selene. The island's flora and fauna whispered secrets of survival—how to find sustenance, seek shelter, and harness the elements. As she explored her surroundings, she felt a connection to the earth that transcended her grief. Each sunrise brought renewed hope, each starry night a reminder of the vast universe that cradled her sorrow. In embracing nature, Selene discovered that healing is not linear; it ebbs and flows like the tides, inviting her to honor her emotions while also pushing her to adapt and grow.

In the solitude of her new reality, Selene began to reflect on the intricate tapestry of family dynamics in survival narratives. The stories of others who had faced adversity resonated with her, reinforcing the idea that love can flourish even in the harshest of circumstances. She envisioned her family's strength, the laughter shared around the dinner table, and the lessons learned in times of struggle. These memories became her compass, guiding her through the uncertainty of her journey. As she navigated the challenges of survival, she felt her father's spirit urging her to embrace resilience, adaptability, and the unwavering bonds of family.

Ultimately, "Carrying Lessons Forward" is a testament to the enduring power of love in the face of loss. Selene's journey on the deserted island is not just about physical survival; it is about nurturing the memories of her past while forging a hopeful future. Each step taken on the sand is a promise to herself and her father—a promise to live fully, to embrace the lessons learned, and to honor the love that transcends life and death. In this sea of shadows, she found the strength to rise, carrying forward the legacy of her Papa, forever anchored in her heart.

Reflections on Loss

Cherishing Memories

In the heart of the tempest, as the waves roared and the winds howled, Selene found herself in a surreal landscape of loss and grief. Her father, once a pillar of strength, now lay still beneath the warm grains of beach sand, a gentle reminder of the love they shared. In that moment, surrounded by the vastness of the ocean and the solitude of the deserted island, she felt the weight of memories pressing upon her heart. Each cherished moment spent with him—laughing, learning, exploring—came flooding back, illuminating the darkness of her despair. It was through these memories that she discovered a flicker of hope, a beacon guiding her through the shadows of her sorrow.

The island became a sanctuary for Selene, a place where the whispers of the past intertwined with the present. As she wandered along the shoreline, the rhythmic sound of the waves echoed the laughter they had shared. Every shell she picked up, every footprint she left in the sand, became a tribute to the bond they had forged. In the silence of nature, she found solace, as if the very essence of her father lingered in the salty breeze and the gentle rustle of palm fronds. Cherishing these memories was not merely an act of remembrance, but a vital survival strategy, allowing her to draw strength from the love that enveloped her.

Survival on this deserted island was not just about finding food and shelter; it was also about nurturing the emotional landscape within her. Selene learned to weave her father's lessons into each day, transforming her grief into resilience. She recalled his teachings about foraging and fishing, applying them with a newfound determination. Each successful catch was a celebration, a moment where the essence of her father lived on in her actions. By actively engaging with her memories, she forged a connection that transcended loss, reminding her that love could endure even in the face of overwhelming adversity.

Family dynamics took on a profound significance in this extreme situation. Alone, yet encumbered with the weight of her memories, Selene grappled with the duality of her experience. The isolation of the island mirrored the emotional chasm created by her father's absence. Yet, within that solitude, she began to understand the importance of resilience and the inherent strength found in familial love. The lessons of cooperation, trust, and courage her father had instilled in her became her lifelines, reinforcing her resolve to survive not just for herself, but as a testament to his enduring spirit.

As days turned into weeks, Selene embraced her surroundings, allowing nature to play its healing role. The vibrant hues of the sunset became a canvas for her reflections, each twilight serving as a reminder of her father's unwavering love. She discovered that in cherishing memories, she was not merely clinging to the past but forging a path toward the future. With the ocean as her witness and the island as her refuge, Selene transformed her sorrow into strength. In the sea of shadows, she began to see the light, a promise that love, once shared, can never truly be lost.

THE IMPACT OF GRIEF

Grief, an emotion as vast and unpredictable as the ocean itself, often overwhelms those who encounter it, especially in the wake of profound loss. For Selene, perched beside her Papa's body, the weight of sorrow is compounded by the desolation of their surroundings. Stranded on a deserted island, the stark reality of her situation becomes painfully clear. The crashing waves echo her heartache, each surge a reminder of the love that was and the life that now feels impossibly distant. In this moment, grief is not just an emotion; it is a force that shapes her very existence, urging her to confront the fragility of life and the strength that lies within her.

As Selene grapples with her loss, the dynamics of her family come into sharp focus. The bond between a daughter and her father is irreplaceable, and the void left by his passing ripples through her memories. Each recollection is tinged with both warmth and despair, illustrating the profound impact that family relationships have in times of crisis. Survival on the island demands not only physical resilience but also emotional fortitude. Selene must learn to navigate her grief while drawing upon the love and lessons her father imparted. In this struggle, she discovers that the shared experiences of loss can either bind families together or tear them apart, depending on how they choose to honor the memories of those they've lost.

Nature, with its relentless cycles of life and death, offers a unique backdrop for healing. The island, though initially a site of despair, begins to reveal its potential for renewal. As Selene observes the resilience of the flora and fauna around her, she starts to understand that grief can coexist with the beauty of life. The birds soaring overhead, the vibrant colors of the sunset, and the sound of the waves crashing against the shore remind her that while loss is profound, it is also part of a larger tapestry of existence. Nature becomes a silent partner in her journey, teaching her that healing is not linear but rather a series of ebbs and flows, much like the tides.

In her quest for survival, Selene discovers practical strategies that intertwine with her emotional healing. Gathering food, finding shelter, and creating tools become acts of remembrance, each task infused with the spirit of her father. As she engages with her environment, she learns to blend her grief with a determination to thrive. The act of survival becomes a tribute to the love they shared, a way for her to keep his memory alive while forging her own path. This interplay between survival and remembrance demonstrates that even in the darkest moments, hope can emerge from despair when we channel our pain into purposeful action.

Ultimately, the impact of grief transforms Selene in ways she could never have anticipated. As she navigates the complexities of loss and survival, she discovers inner strength and resilience. The island, once a symbol of her despair, becomes a sanctuary for growth and reflection. Through the process of grieving, Selene learns that love endures beyond the physical presence of a loved one. It becomes a guiding light, illuminating her path as she learns to embrace life again. In this journey through grief, she finds not only a way to honor her father but also a renewed sense of purpose, a testament to the enduring power of love in the face of unimaginable loss.

Transforming Pain into Purpose

In the heart of despair, where the horizon blurs between grief and hope, Selene found herself on the deserted shore, the weight of her father's absence pressing down on her. The storm that had stolen their boat had also taken her anchor in life, leaving her adrift in a sea of shadows. Yet, in this profound moment of loss, a flicker of resilience began to ignite within her. Surrounded by the vastness of the ocean and the whispering winds, Selene understood that transforming her pain into purpose would be the only way to honor her father's memory and navigate the treacherous waters ahead.

As she sat beside her Papa, the grains of sand clinging to his still form, Selene contemplated the lessons he had imparted. He had always spoken of survival not just as a physical endeavor but as a spiritual journey. To survive was to adapt, to learn from the environment, and to harness the beauty around them. In her solitude, she realized that the wilderness offered more than mere resources; it held the key to healing. Each crashing wave echoed her sorrow, but with every tide, she felt a surge of determination to rise above her anguish and channel it into something meaningful.

The island, once a backdrop to her family's adventures, transformed into a sanctuary of reflection. As Selene explored its hidden treasures, she began to weave her grief into the fabric of her surroundings. The vibrant flora, the rhythmic calls of the birds, and the salty breeze became her companions in solitude. Each day, she devoted time to learning the rhythms of nature, using her experiences to build shelter, gather food, and create a safe haven, not just for herself but as a tribute to the love she shared with her father. In doing so, she discovered that her pain was not a burden but a catalyst for growth and resilience.

Selene's journey was a poignant exploration of family dynamics in the face of adversity. The loss of her father created a chasm in her heart, yet it also revealed the strength inherited from their bond. Memories flooded her mind, reminding her of the laughter they shared and the lessons he instilled in her. As she faced the challenges of survival, Selene began to feel his presence in the rustling leaves and the gentle sway of the palm trees. Each challenge she overcame became a testament to their enduring connection, fueling her resolve to not only survive but to thrive in this newfound solitude.

Ultimately, Selene's transformation became a narrative of hope for others who might find themselves in similar predicaments. Her journey illustrated that pain, while overwhelming, can be reframed into purpose through the lens of nature's healing power. As she stood on the shore, watching the sun dip below the horizon, she realized that her father's legacy lived on through her courage and tenacity. In the embrace of the wild, she found the strength to turn her sorrow into a beacon of light, guiding her through the shadows and onto a path of rediscovery, resilience, and profound love.

A New Beginning

Embracing Change

Change is a constant force, sweeping through our lives like the tides that kiss the shores of the deserted island where Selene finds herself. Stranded and grappling with the profound loss of her father, she is thrust into an unforgiving reality that challenges every aspect of her existence. In moments of despair, it is essential to embrace change, not as a foe but as a catalyst for growth and resilience. The island, with its wild beauty and harshness, becomes a teacher, revealing the strength that lies within her and the importance of adapting to new circumstances.

Survival strategies in extreme situations often highlight the need for both physical and emotional transformation. For Selene, survival is not merely about finding food and shelter; it is also about navigating her grief and the shifting dynamics of her family unit, now irrevocably altered. The lessons learned from her father's unwavering spirit encourage her to harness her instincts. She begins to see how each challenge—whether it's building a shelter from palm fronds or foraging for edible plants—requires her to change her approach and mindset. Embracing change becomes a guiding principle, allowing her to honor her father's legacy while carving out her own path.

The family dynamics in survival narratives are complex, often revealing the best and worst in people. In the face of adversity, Selene discovers the depths of her own character and the bonds that tie her to her father. Although he is physically gone, the memories they shared and the lessons he imparted become a source of strength. She learns to communicate with the echoes of his wisdom, transforming her grief into motivation. This internal dialogue fosters resilience, illustrating how embracing change helps one to navigate the labyrinth of loss and love, ultimately leading to a deeper understanding of oneself.

Nature plays a pivotal role in Selene's healing journey. The island, initially a symbol of isolation, transforms into a sanctuary where she can process her emotions. The rhythm of the waves, the rustle of the leaves, and the vibrant colors of the sunsets remind her of the beauty that still exists amidst her pain. Each day brings new opportunities to connect with her surroundings, offering solace and a reminder that life continues, even in the face of tragedy. By embracing change, she learns to find peace in the chaos, discovering that healing often requires a willingness to let go of the past and welcome the future with open arms.

As Selene adapts to her new reality, she embodies the spirit of resilience that defines human survival. Embracing change becomes her lifeline, guiding her through the dark moments of despair and lighting her path toward healing. In this journey, she learns that while loss is an indelible part of life, change is the force that can transform that loss into something beautiful. Through the lens of her experience, readers are reminded that embracing change is not merely an act of survival; it is a profound journey toward understanding, growth, and ultimately, love.

THE LEGACY OF LOVE

In the heart of despair, love serves as a beacon, illuminating even the darkest corners of grief. For Selene, perched beside her Papa's body on the sun-drenched shore, the weight of loss was overwhelming. Yet, amidst the sorrow, memories of shared laughter and warmth enveloped her like a protective cocoon. Their bond, forged through countless adventures and whispers of the wind, became her lifeline. As she gazed at the horizon, where the sun kissed the sea, Selene understood that love transcends physical presence; it transforms into an enduring legacy, guiding her steps forward.

Survival on a deserted island demanded more than just physical strength; it required an unwavering spirit and an unbreakable bond with those we hold dear. Selene recalled the lessons her Papa imparted during their family expeditions, teaching her to read the signs of nature and listen to its rhythms. In the face of adversity, these teachings became her survival strategies. She crafted tools from the remnants of their boat, foraged for food, and built a shelter, all while feeling her father's love enveloping her, urging her to carry on. Love, in its purest form, became the foundation of her resilience, fueling her determination to survive not just for herself but in honor of him.

Family dynamics shift dramatically in the crucible of survival. In this isolated world, Selene's memories of her Papa became her compass, steering her through the storm of emotions that threatened to engulf her. She found strength in their shared history, each memory a thread woven into the fabric of her identity. The lessons they had learned together echoed in her mind, reminding her of the importance of hope and perseverance. Even in solitude, she was never truly alone; her father's spirit danced in the waves, whispered through the rustling palm leaves, and shone brightly in the stars above.

Nature, a fierce yet nurturing force, played a crucial role in Selene's healing journey. The island, with its lush greenery and endless ocean, became both a sanctuary and a classroom. As she learned to navigate its challenges, the beauty around her offered moments of solace. Each sunrise painted the sky with hues of resilience, while the rhythmic crashing of waves became a lullaby, soothing her aching heart. In the embrace of nature, Selene discovered that healing is not linear; it ebbs and flows, much like the tides, and through this ebbing, she began to piece together the fragments of her brokenness.

In the end, the legacy of love Selene inherited became the guiding force that shaped her path forward. Though her Papa was gone, the love they shared continued to pulse within her, a reminder of the strength that can be drawn from the bonds of family. It was this love that urged her to embrace life again, to find joy in the small miracles of each day. As she stood on the shore, with the waves lapping at her feet, Selene vowed to carry forth their story, allowing the legacy of love to ripple through the lives she would touch. In a world shadowed by loss, love emerged as a powerful force, illuminating the way toward healing and survival.

Moving Forward Together

In the aftermath of unimaginable loss, Selene sat quietly on the sandy shore, her heart heavy yet resilient. The waves whispered secrets of the island, each crash against the rocks echoing the raw emotion of her grief. She found herself perched beside her Papa, the man who had taught her the ways of the sea and the importance of family. Covered in the soft beach sand, he seemed at peace, a stark contrast to the turmoil swirling within her. In that moment, Selene understood that moving forward together meant embracing not only the memories of those lost but also the bonds that remained unbroken among the living.

Survival on the deserted island was not merely a test of physical endurance but an exploration of the intricate dynamics of family. As Selene navigated her new reality, she leaned on the teachings imparted by her father. With every sunrise, she gathered the strength to face the challenges ahead, directing her grief into practical strategies that ensured her and her family's survival. They worked together, scavenging for food, building shelter, and finding solace in each other's presence. Each task became a tribute to her Papa, a way to honor his memory while forging an unbreakable bond with her family.

Nature played an integral role in their healing process. The vibrant flora and fauna surrounding them acted as both a refuge and a source of inspiration. Selene learned to observe and respect the rhythms of the island, understanding that life thrives even in the harshest conditions. The nurturing embrace of the sun and the soothing sounds of the ocean became a balm for her aching heart. Through the lens of survival, Selene began to appreciate the beauty of resilience, recognizing that the natural world held lessons in grief and renewal.

As days turned into weeks, Selene found strength in the shared experiences of her family. They laughed, cried, and celebrated small victories together, each moment reinforcing their collective will to survive. The island, once a symbol of isolation, transformed into a sacred space where they could confront their sorrow and emerge stronger. Together, they crafted a new narrative, one woven with threads of love, loss, and an unwavering commitment to each other. It was in these shared moments that Selene learned moving forward together meant embracing vulnerability and finding solace in the support of her loved ones.

Ultimately, moving forward together became a testament to the enduring spirit of family. Selene's journey was not just about physical survival; it was about emotional healing and the recognition that even in the face of despair, hope could flourish. The bonds forged in adversity would guide her through the darkest nights and brightest days. With each new dawn, as she looked out across the horizon, Selene felt her Papa's spirit alongside her, urging her to embrace life in all its complexity. Together, they would navigate the sea of shadows and emerge into the light, hand in hand, heart to heart.

www.ingramcontent.com/pod-product-compliance
Lightning Source LLC
LaVergne TN
LVHW010504160826
845677LV00012B/2650

* 9 7 9 8 8 9 5 6 9 7 8 4 9 *